ARGYLE

Barbara Brooks Wallace

Illustrated by John Sandford

BELL BOOKS

For
Jimmy of Clan Wallace
with love and the usual ten—BBW

For
Kathryn Jo Ames
From me to ewe—JS

....

Published by Bell Books
Boyds Mills Press, Inc.
A Highlights Company
910 Church Street
Honesdale, Pennsylvania 18431

Publisher Cataloging-in-Publication Data
Wallace, Barbara Brooks
Argyle / Barbara Brooks Wallace ; illustrated by John Sandford
[32] p. : col. ill. ; cm.
Originally published by Abingdon Press, Nashville, 1987
Summary: A Scottish sheep's unusual diet causes him to produce
multicolored wool, which changes his life and his owners' fortune.
ISBN 1-56397-043-0
1. Sheep—Fiction—Juvenile literature. (1. Sheep—Fiction.)
I. Sandford, John, ill. II. Title.
[F]   1992
Library of Congress Catalog Card Number: 91-76021

Book designed by John R. Robinson
Distributed by St. Martin's Press
Printed in Hong Kong

Once upon a time, somewhere in Scotland, there was a sheep whose name was Argyle.

Argyle was exactly like all the other sheep. He looked like a sheep, and he felt like a sheep. He liked to do the same things other sheep did. He wasn't one bit different from any of them, and he didn't give a *hoot mon* about it.

When MacDougal the sheepherder herded his sheep into the pen to shear their wool for market, he couldn't tell Argyle from the rest of them.

"A sheep is a sheep," MacDougal always said. "They're all the same."

That was all right with Argyle. It was exactly the way he wanted it.

All day with the rest of MacDougal's sheep, Argyle roamed the highlands and the lowlands and the middle lands. It was peaceful and quiet. It was exactly the way he wanted it.

Sheep like to go around in bunches. So did Argyle. But once in a while a sheep likes to wander away from the others. So did Argyle. He didn't do it very often. Just sometimes.

One day he wandered off and came to a place behind some tall rocks where he had never been before. The grass there tasted really good. So did some strange little flowers with red and blue and white and green and purple and yellow petals. In fact, they were outstanding.

Argyle didn't tell anyone about them. But the next day he quietly wandered back. And the day after that. And the day after that. He ate hundreds of the little colored flowers.

One day MacDougal's wife,
Katharine, said, "Why dinna ye tell me
about the many-colored sheep,
MacDougal?"

"Because we do na have a many-
colored sheep, Katharine," said
MacDougal.

"Look again," said Katharine.

MacDougal looked again and saw that they did indeed have a many-colored sheep. Its wool was red and blue and white and green and purple and yellow. The sheep was Argyle.

MacDougal ran for his shears and started clipping. Katharine ran for her knitting needles and started knitting.

Then they both ran to show all their friends and neighbors the socks Katharine had knit. They were a beautiful plaid. Well! You can imagine what a sensation a sheep who grew wool that knit into *plaid* socks would be in Scotland. Argyle became famous overnight.

It didn't take MacDougal long to decide that Argyle should not be wandering around with the rest of the sheep, so he put Argyle in a pen by himself where he was all alone. Except for the hundreds of people who paid a lot of money to come and see him. And to buy some of his wool. They paid a lot of money for that, too. Soon MacDougal and Katharine grew very rich. Mayor Loch of Lomond came out and gave Argyle a medal.

But Argyle felt as if he weren't a sheep anymore. He was just a public exhibition. He hated it. It was never peaceful and quiet. He couldn't roam the highlands and the lowlands and the middle lands. And, of course, he couldn't get back to the place where the pretty little colored flowers grew. So he started to turn sheep color again.

MacDougal was so worried that he fed Argyle all kinds of vitamins and minerals and terrible-tasting food. It made Argyle miserable.

Soon he not only stopped *feeling* like a sheep, he stopped *looking* like one, too, because all his wool fell out. Well! It didn't take long for the people to stop coming around. Except for Mayor Loch of Lomond, who came to take away the medal.

Fortunately, he couldn't take away MacDougal's money, so MacDougal and Katharine stayed rich the rest of their days. Katharine kept right on knitting and finally discovered a way to make plaid socks out of different bits of dyed wool. She called them Argyle socks, of course. You may have heard of them.

MacDougal finally gave up on Argyle and sent him out with the rest of the sheep. Argyle grew back his old sheep coat, and soon you couldn't tell him from any other sheep. He looked like a sheep and he felt like a sheep again.

As for the place with the pretty colored flowers, if Argyle ever went back there, he never told anyone. And he stayed his plain old sheep color, so you could be pretty sure he wasn't eating anything but the grass.

He just roamed the highlands and the lowlands and the middle lands with all the other sheep. It was peaceful and quiet. It was exactly the way he wanted it.